Happy Mother's Day, Mami!

by Leslie Valdes
illustrated by the Jason Fruchter

Simon Spotlight/Nick Jr.

New York   London   Toronto   Sydney   Singapore

Visit us at abdopublishing.com

Spotlight Library bound edition © 2007. Spotlight is a division of ABDO Publishing Company, Edina, Minnesota.

Simon Spotlight

An Imprint of Simon & Schuster Children's Publishing Division
1230 Avenue of the Americas, New York, New York 10020

ISBN-13 978-1-59961-242-3 (reinforced library bound edition)
ISBN-10 1-59961-242-9 (reinforced library bound edition)

Library of Congress Cataloging-In-Publication Data

This book was previously cataloged with the following information:

Valdes, Leslie
Happy Mother's Day, Mami! / by Leslie Valdes ; illustrated by Jason Fruchter.
  p. cm. (Dora the Exporer ; #3)
ISBN 0-689-85233-9
Summary: It's Mother's Day! Dora has decided to make a special cake for her mami, but first she must gather all the ingredients.
  [1. Dora the explorer (Fictitious character)--Fiction. 2. Mother's Day--Fiction. 3. Cake--Fiction.] I. Title. II. Series: Dora the Explorer ; #3.
  PZ7.V215 Ha 2003
  [Fic]--dc22

2003278506

Today is Mother's Day! *¡El Día de las Madres!* I'm making a special cake for my *mami*. Will you help me make the cake? Great!

First we need to find the recipe card for the banana-nut-chocolate cake. Do you see the recipe card that has bananas, nuts, and chocolate?

Here's the recipe card! But where can we find bananas, nuts, and chocolate? Let's ask the Map. Say, "Map!"

Map says we have to go to the Banana Grove, then through the Nutty Forest, and finally to the Chocolate Tree! Then we'll have all the ingredients to make my *mami's* cake.

Look! It's my friend Boots the monkey!
Boots drew a picture for his mommy for Mother's Day.

Come on, let's go to the Banana Grove! Do you see the grove?

We made it to the Banana Grove. We need three bananas for the cake. The bananas need to be yellow—that means they're ripe! Do you see three yellow bananas?

Good counting!

Hey, look, it's our friend Benny the bull. Hi, Benny! He gave a cowbell to his grandma for Mother's Day. What a nice gift!

¡*Vámonos!* Let's go to the Nutty Forest. We still have to get the other ingredients. Bye, Benny!

Here we are at the Nutty Forest. And there's our friend Tico the squirrel. He's giving his mommy a bracelet made of nuts for Mother's Day. It's so pretty.

We need to collect six nuts. Let's count them in Spanish: *uno, dos, tres, cuatro, cinco, seis!*

You did it! Good counting!

Hey, look, it's our friend Isa the iguana. Hi, Isa!
Isa is gathering flowers to give to her mommy for
Mother's Day.

Oh, no! Look! There's Swiper the fox. That sneaky fox is trying to swipe Isa's flowers. Say, "Swiper, no swiping!"

You did it! You saved Isa's flowers! Now we have to go to the Chocolate Tree. Do you see the Chocolate Tree?

Come on, let's go get the last ingredient for my *mami's* special cake!

We made it to the Chocolate Tree! It only has one piece of chocolate left, and it's way up high. Can you help us reach it? Put your hands in the air and reach really high!

Yay! You reached the chocolate! Now we have all the ingredients. Let's go home and make the cake.

This is my daddy, *mi papi*. He's going to help us make the cake. First we put all the ingredients into a bowl and mix them up. *Bate, bate, bate!* Mix, mix, mix!

After we mix all the ingredients *Papi* will put the cake in the oven to bake. The cake will be ready soon. Thanks for helping!

It's time to give my *mami* the special cake!

Mami says it's delicious—¡delicioso!

Happy Mother's Day, *Mami!*